D1192482

More titles from Finding My Way Books

I Want To Be Like Poppin' Joe
I Don't Know If I Want a Puppy
Kaitlyn Wants To See Ducks
Marco and I Want To Play Ball
MyaGrace Wants To Make Music
Reese Has a Halloween Secret
OE Wants It To Be Friday

Copyright © 2016 Finding My Way Books
All rights reserved.
ISBN: 978-0-9968357-9-4

MyaGrace Wants To Get Ready

Finding My Way Books

true stories of inclusion and
the development of skills
needed for self-determination

By Jo Meserve Mach and
Vera Lynne Stroup-Rentier

Photography by Mary Birdsell

Our reason for sharing this story...

MyaGrace was adopted from India to the US when she was two years old. She was very small for her age and had difficulty eating. Today she is an enthusiastic teenager wanting to experience life as fully as possible.

MyaGrace has Cerebral Palsy, Autism and intellectual disabilities. Her family helps support her in the activities she chooses. MyaGrace loves activities that involve music and dancing. As a result, she wanted to go to the school dance.

We chose to write this story because it demonstrates how teenage girls with disabilities want to be included in activities with their friends and classmates, just like every teenager out there. With support that is encouraging and respectful, MyaGrace shows us how she is learning skills needed for her self-determination. She fully participates in plans and goals that she needs to complete in order to be ready for her dance.

We wish to share with you the pure joy that is revealed in this story,
~Jo, Vera and Mary

A True Story Promoting
Inclusion and Self-Determination

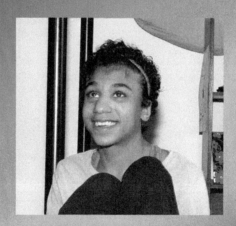

Finding My Way Books is dedicated to celebrating the success
of inclusion by sharing stories about children with
special needs in families and communities.

For more information:
www.findingmywaybooks.com

Hi, my name is MyaGrace.
My family and I like music.
We listen to music all the time.

I like dance music the best.
I love to dance.
My brother, Ethan, likes to dance with me.

My friend, Emily, sent me a message.
There's going to be a dance at school.
I want to go.
I'll ask Mom.

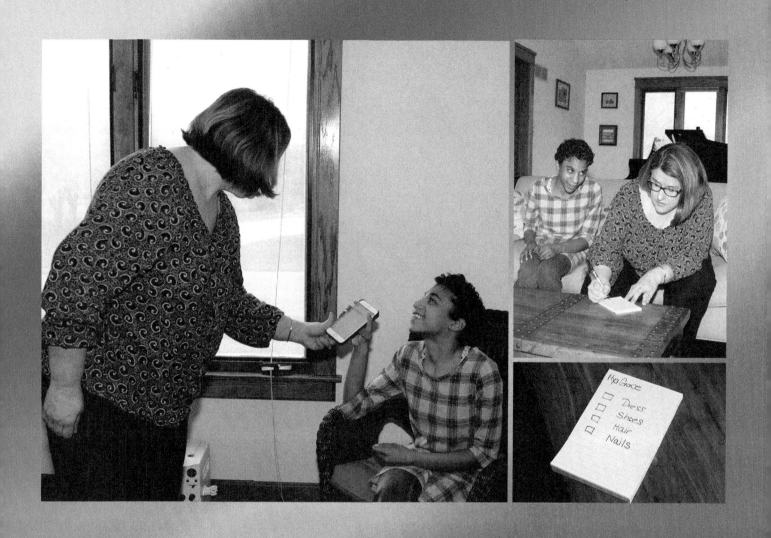

Mom says I can go.
Hooray!
Now I need to get ready.
Mom helps me make a list.

"MyaGrace, I borrowed some dresses.
Are you ready to try them on?"
"Just a minute, I'll get ready."

I show Mom the dress I like.
She says it's too big.
That's okay.
I'll pick another dress.

I'll be cold in this one.
I can't walk in this one.

I like this color.
It's purple and it shines.
I can't wait to tell Emily about my dress.

I want to practice dancing in my dress.
"Ethan, come dance."

What else do I need to get ready?
I check my list.

"MyaGrace, I have some new shoes.
Are you ready to try them on?"
"Just a minute, I'll get ready."

I show Mom the boots I like.
She says they aren't dress shoes.
I need to pick different shoes.

These shoes are pretty.
The color goes with my dress.

Can I dance in these shoes?
I need to practice.
"Ethan, will you dance with me again?"

15

I like these shoes.
I can dance in them.
I need to show Emily.
Mom is trying to take a picture.

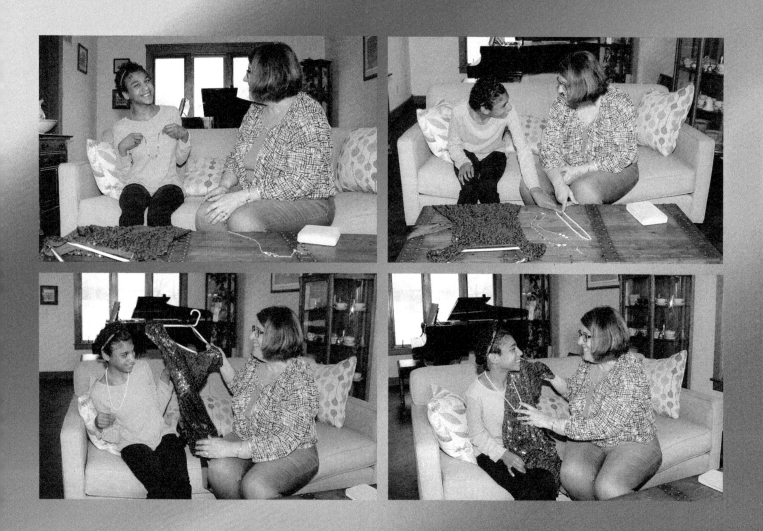

I pick out what else I want to wear.
This will help me get ready.

Now I know what comes next.
Hair and nails are what I like best.

The dance is tonight.
Lori is going to help me get ready.

I love coming to Lori's shop.
I like to help Lori.
Mom gets her hair done first.

Now I need to pick my nail color.
There are so many colors.
I found it!

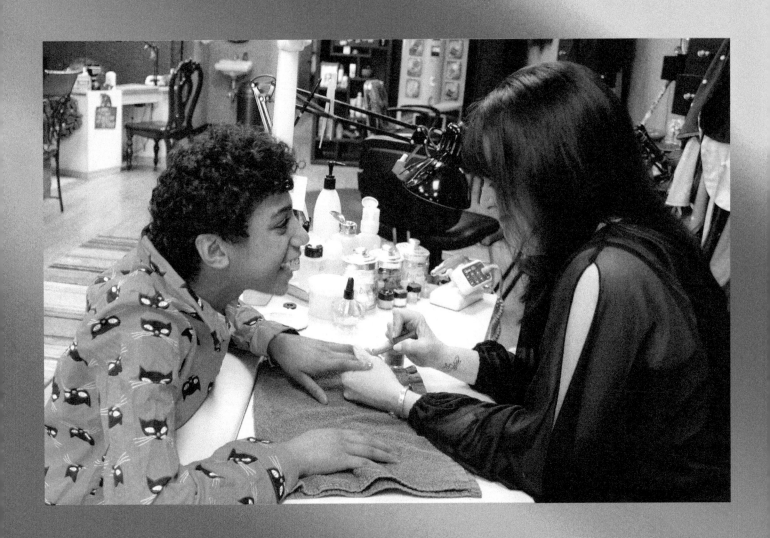

"It looks good.
Thank you, Lori."

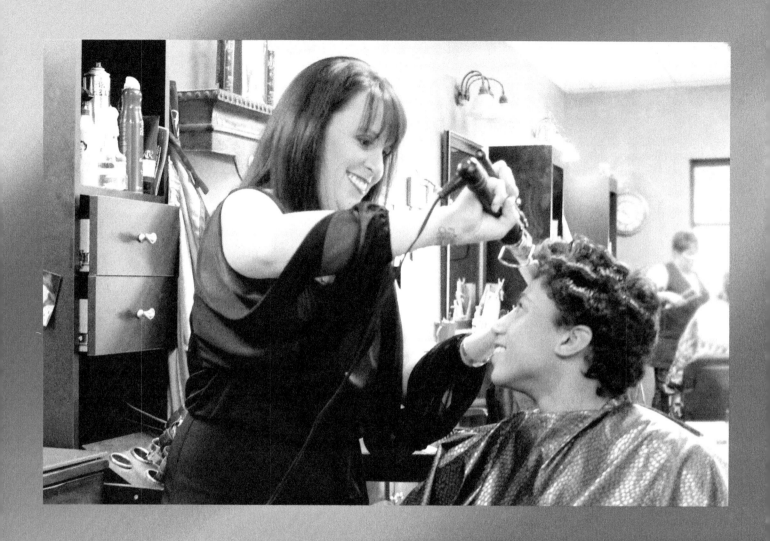

It's time to do my hair.

"How does it look?"
Lori says my hair looks good.
I like it!

Mom and Lori have a surprise for me.
I'm getting makeup.

"Are we done yet?"
Lori says we're not done yet.
"I love it already!"

I want my lipstick just like Lori's.
"Thank you, Lori, for doing my makeup."
I love makeup.
What a great surprise.

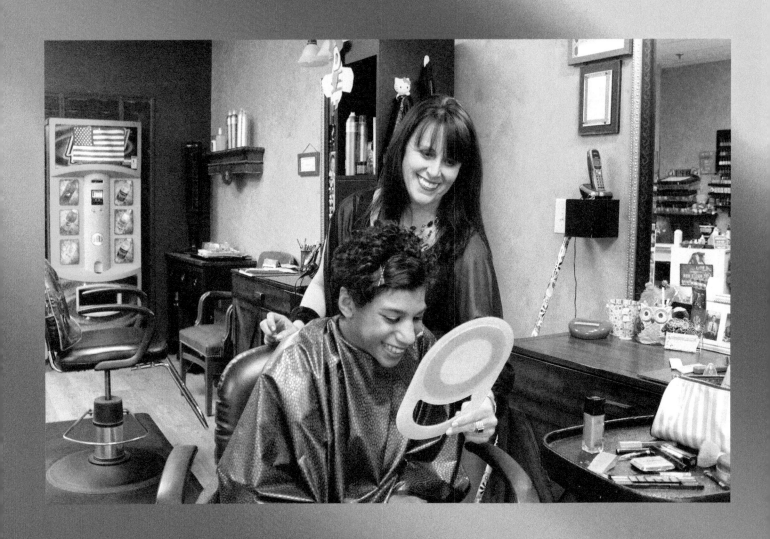

I look great!

My list is done.
I've got to go home and get ready.

Emily is coming over soon.
I'm ready to dance!

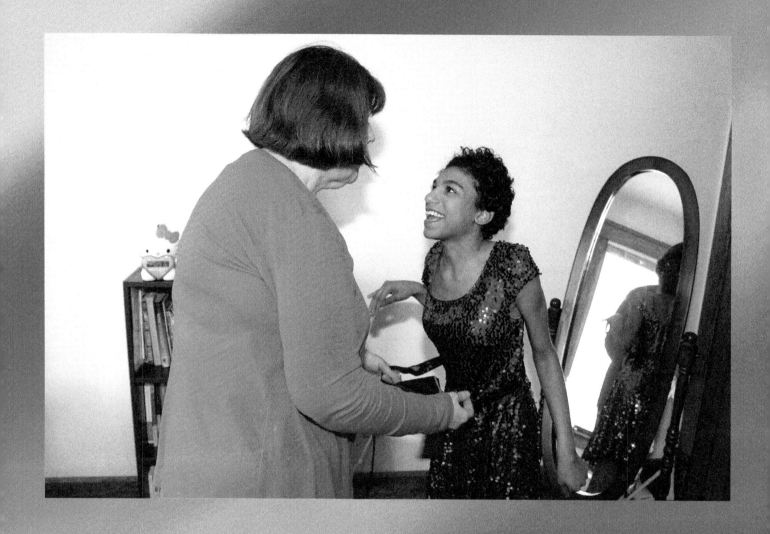

Mom is good at helping.
I'm almost ready.

I want to finish by myself.
Now I'm ready.

"MyaGrace, Emily's here.
Are you ready?"

We're ready!

Thank you to MyaGrace, her family and friends for sharing their story.

MyaGrace wants you to know she danced every dance
and had a wonderful time at her school dance.

'MyaGrace Wants To Get Ready' Index

Skills promoting self-determination are seen in this book:

Encouraging self-determination skill building in children

Our books are written in the actual voice of a child. The child is telling their story of how they are learning to be more self-determined.

Here are examples of self-determination skills:
1. Choice making
2. Decision making
3. Problem solving
4. Goal setting and planning
5. Self-direction behaviors (self-regulation)
6. Responsibility
7. Independence
8. Self-awareness and self-knowledge
9. Self-advocacy and leadership
10. Communication
11. Participation
12. Having relationships and social connections

Weir, K., Cooney, M., Walter, M., Moss, C., & Carter, E. W. (2011). Fostering self-determination among children with disabilities: Ideas from parents for parents. *Madison, WI: Natural Supports Project, Waisman Center, University of Wisconsin—Madison.*

Family Guide for Promoting Self-Determination

When MyaGrace asked her mom if she could attend her school dance her mom could have said yes and made all the plans for her. Instead, her mom included her fully in the preparation plans. As a result there were multiple opportunities for MyaGrace to gain the skills she needs for self-determination.

Encourage choice making:
MyaGrace is asked to make choices and these choices are honored. MyaGrace chose that she wanted to go to the dance, the shoes and dress she would wear, and the color of her nail polish. It is helpful to support your child as they make choices.

Encourage decision making:
MyaGrace actively participated in making the decision of which dress she would wear to the dance. She determined that one dress made her cold and one was too long. She made the decision that she would wear the purple, shiny dress.

Encourage participation:
MyaGrace was not told what to wear to the dance. She fully participated in the choosing process by trying on the dresses and thinking about each one. She also participated in choosing her shoes, jewelry, and nail polish. She loves participating with her friends at the school dance.

Encourage problem solving:
MyaGrace realized that winter boots were not the best match for her dress. She also asked her brother, Ethan, to help her practice dancing in her dress so she would be ready for her school dance.

Encourage relationships
MyaGrace has a friendship with Emily. Her brother, Ethan, is her dance partner at home. She has a special relationship with Lori, who cuts her hair regularly.

Encourage high interest activities:
Going to the school dance is a 'dream activity' for MyaGrace. She loves music and dancing. She loves getting her hair, nails and makeup done.

Encourage goal setting:
MyaGrace's mother helped her make a list so she had goals to complete to be ready for her dance. MyaGrace marked off the items on her list as she completed those goals.

Encourage self-direction and independence:
MyaGrace shows her mom the boots she could wear to the dance. She shares her dress and shoes with Lori. She helps Lori at her beauty shop. She practices dancing so she is ready for her school dance.

Encourage self-awareness:
MyaGrace loves her nail polish, hair-do and makeup. She knows she looks great.

Classroom Activities for 'MyaGrace Wants To Get Ready'

1. Facilitating problem solving:
Have each student make a list of five or more things they need to complete to be ready to come to school in the morning. Facilitate a discussion and have the class identify two things they could change to be more successful in getting ready in the morning.   For example: a student chooses what they are going to wear to school the night before.

2. Facilitating decision making:
Have students plan a dance for their class. Have them make a list of what they need to accomplish to have a fun dance. They will need to make many decisions such as: when to have the dance, where to have the dance, what music they should play, etc.

3. Facilitating self-direction:
Have students identify one thing they could do for another person to help them be ready for a special activity. In this story Ethan helps MyaGrace practice dancing, her mom borrows dresses for her to try on, and Lori fixes her hair, nails and makeup.

*true stories of inclusion and
the development of skills
needed for self-determination*

Jo Meserve Mach, author and publisher, spent 36 years as an Occupational Therapist. She is very passionate about sharing the stories of children with special needs. Jo embraces the joy that individuals with disabilities bring to our communities through their unique gifts.

Vera Lynne Stroup-Rentier, author, was an Early Childhood and Special Education teacher and trainer for 25 years. She has a PhD in Special Education from the University of Kansas and is currently working at the Kansas State Department of Education. Vera is passionate about the inclusion of each and every child in settings where they would be if they did not have a disability. Parenting a teen and tween with special needs enrich her life.

Mary Birdsell is a freelance photographer and a former Speech and Theatre teacher. She strives to create images that reflect the strengths of each child. Mary's background in education, theatre and photography intersect as she visually creates our books. She uses colors and shapes to tell a story. For her, each book is like it's own theatrical production.

MyaGrace Rentier is a middle school student. She loves music and has a gift for enthusiasm. MyaGrace demonstrated her self-advocacy skills by telling her mother that she would like to talk about books to help our team. Today she shares her gift of enthusiasm by helping promote all our 'Finding My Way' books.

For more information about all of our
titles and to purchase books:
www.findingmywaybooks.com

Contact us at:
findingmywaybooks@gmail.com

CPSIA information can be obtained
at www.ICGtesting.com
Printed in the USA
LVOW05s1306300416

486060LV00006B/18/P